D1191813

Marsha Parish

Copyright © 2022 Marsha Parish

All rights reserved.

o oo oooo ooooooo oooo oo

DEDICATION

This story was inspired by my
upbringing in Louisiana, and its
unique traditions, diverse culture,
and vibrant atmosphere.

My very own Memaw taught me
how to make a great gumbo, as well
as other important life lessons.

I dedicate this book in her memory.

o oo oooo ooooooo oooo oo

o oo oooo ooooooo oooo oo

Life Is Like Gumbo

o oo oooo oooooooo oooo oo

It was quiet throughout the house, and the purple room down the hall was in darkness.

Mya could only see her little blue butterfly night-light glowing brightly by the wall.

o oo oooo ooooooo oooo oo o

It was past her bedtime,

but she was wide awake.

Mya was too excited to sleep.

She just couldn't stop

thinking about her big trip.

You see, she was leaving in

the morning to visit her

Memaw down in New Orleans.

o oo oooo ooooooo oooo oo

Memaw is Mya's

grandma from the

state of Louisiana.

. . ..

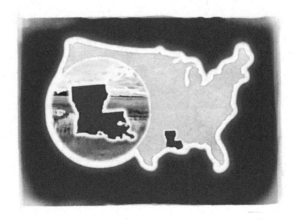

On a map of the world,
Louisiana is on the continent
of North America, and is one
of fifty states that form the
United States of America.

On a map of the United States,
Louisiana is located in the
South, between the states of
Mississippi and Texas, and just
below the state of Arkansas.

o oo oooo oooooooo oooo oo

o oo oooo ooooooooo oooo oo o

Louisiana is different from all other states because it is the only one with parishes, instead of counties.

o oo oooo ooooooooo oooo oo o

Mya's parents were both from Saint Bernard Parish, but moved to the state of Oklahoma after the destruction caused by a powerful hurricane, named Katrina, in 2005.

o oo oooo ooooooooo oooo oo

She didn't visit Louisiana as often as she'd like, but seemed to learn something new about the area each time that she did. It was carnival time when Mya last visited New Orleans.

And for the first time, she got the chance to catch beads and other throws from big, colorful floats during the biggest parade of the season!

o oo oooo oooooooo oooo oo

Mardi Gras is what it's called, but it is also known as Fat Tuesday, because that's what it translates to in the French language.

o oo oooo ooooooo oooo oo

The day marks the end of
all **carnival** celebrations
for that year.

Mya remembered having
a blast that day.

But, even more than Mardi
Gras, she enjoyed being in the
kitchen, learning how to bake and
cook by watching her Memaw,
and helping in any way possible.

o oo oooo ooooooo oooo oo

. .. .

Cookies are easy to make,

and were the first
treat that Memaw
taught Mya to bake.

———————————————

They made pralines and
other desserts together last
summer, but Mya liked the
powdery beignets best.

o oo oooo oooooooo oooo oo

Beignets are similar to donuts, but have a squared shape and are typically covered in white powdered sugar.

o oo oooo oooooooo oooo oo

Southern pralines are normally cooked with a mixture of butter, milk, sugar, and pecans.
. . ..

However, chocolate chips were also added into Memaw and Mya's praline recipe.

• •• •• •• • • • •• •• •• •

As she rested in her cozy bed,
Mya's mind was flooded with all
of those wonderful memories.

Before she knew it, she

was fast asleep, dreaming

about the sugary king

cake that they made

together last Mardi Gras.

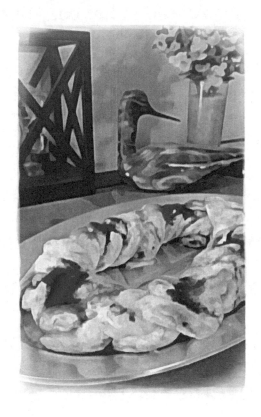

Beeeeeep!

BEEEEEEEEP!

Beeeeeep!

Mya's alarm clock rang out loudly, waking her from the sweet dream that she could almost taste.

The sun had finally risen, and it was morning time.

o oo oooo ooooooooo oooo oo

o oo oooo oooooooo oooo oo o

Mya silenced the noisy
alarm and crawled out from
the warmth of her blanket.

She sat up, stretched out her
arms, and let out a big yawn.

Then, she eagerly swung
her legs over the side and
hopped down onto the
fuzzy rug beside her bed.

o oo oooo oooooooo oooo oo

. .. .

She slid her bare feet into

a pair of soft, black slippers

and went into the bathroom

to get ready for the day.

o oo oooo oooooooo oooo oo

o oo oooo ooooooo oooo oo o

First, she brushed her teeth
and combed her hair.

Next, she went over to the
closet to find her favorite sun-
dress and matching sandals.

Then, she quickly changed,
and headed downstairs to
the kitchen for breakfast.

o oo oooo ooooooo oooo oo

Her mom was flipping the last pancake by the time she sat down at the table.

• •• •• •• •

With one hand around a cup of orange juice, Mya inhaled a deep breath and grinned.

• •• •• •• •

She loved the savory smell of butter and fried batter that filled the air.

o oo oooo ooooooo oooo oo

· · ·· · ·· ·

After breakfast,

Mom asked,

"Ready?"

· · ·· · ·· ·

o oo oooo ooooooo oooo oo

○ ○○ ○○○○ ○○○○○○○○ ○○○○ ○○ ○

Mya grabbed her
bags with excitement

and replied, "Ready!

Let's go see Memaw!"

The trip was long, but

Mya didn't mind.

As they traveled,

she admired the scenery

from the car window.

· ·· ·· ··· ·

She liked crossing over

the many bridges

throughout Louisiana.

Some were **big** and **long**.

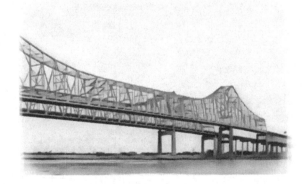

o oo oooo ooooooo oooo oo

Some were **small** and **short**.

Some were **old** and **rusty**.

o oo oooo   oooooooo oooo oo

They even caught one of the

bridges, and waited while

a boat passed underneath.

o oo oooo oooooooo oooo oo

Mya noticed that while each bridge had a different look, they were all built for the same purpose.

Some allowed vehicles to pass over rivers with ships and tugboats. Some allowed vehicles to pass over swamps and lakes with sailboats and airboats.

o oo oooo oooooooo oooo oo

o oo oooo oooooooo oooo oo o

And some allowed vehicles

to pass over small canals

and bayous with crab boats,

oyster boats, and shrimp

boats docked near their shores.

o oo oooo oooooooo oooo oo

Southern crab boats use special box shaped traps with bait to capture crabs.

The traps are thrown into the water to sink down to the bottom. A rope with a floating cork, or buoy, is pulled to bring the trap back up. Any trapped crabs inside get shaken out into boxes.

o oo oooo oooooooo oooo oo

Oyster boats are much larger and can carry many sacks of oysters, totaling hundreds of pounds at a time.

The boats are equipped with dredges, or tongs, that are lowered into the water and dragged along the bottom.

Any oysters caught inside of its baskets are removed and harvested by size afterwards.

o oo oooo oooooooo oooo oo

Trawler boats are

typically tall because

they have huge nets

that are pulled below

the water's surface

to catch seafood,

like shrimp and fish.

o oo oooo ooooooo oooo oo

○ ○○ ○○○○ ○○○○○○○○ ○○○○ ○○ ○

As they drove on, Mya

licked her lips at the

thought of boiled shrimp.

○ ○○ ○○○○ ○○○○○○○○ ○○○○ ○○

But after passing by wetlands with crawfish farms in rice fields, she now longed for them, too.

o oo oooo ooooooo oooo oo o

Mya called them mud bugs because they are known to dig deep down into it to borrow. The mud helps protect the crawfish from the hot sun.

o oo oooo ooooooo oooo oo

They also passed near

swamps with beautiful

oak trees, covered in moss.

Mya even saw a few pelicans and an alligator along the way!

o oo oooo ooooooo oooo oo o

The brown pelican is the official state bird of Louisiana, while the alligator is the state's official reptile.

o oo oooo ooooooo oooo oo

A **pelican** can be seen on Louisiana's state flag, as well.

Eventually, Mya saw the big, round Superdome from the interstate, and knew that they were close to their destination.

. .. .

The Louisiana Superdome is an iconic landmark in New Orleans, and the home stadium of a professional football team called the New Orleans Saints.

Mya had never been to a

football game before, but

hoped to go someday.

o oo oooo ooooooo oooo oo

Not long after passing the Superdome, they turned onto a gravel driveway that lead to Memaw's big blue house.

o oo oooo oooooooo oooo oo o

When they arrived, Memaw was waiting on her front porch with a glass of sweet iced tea.

Mya couldn't wait to exit the car and stretch her legs.

She skipped over to her grandma and embraced her with a warm, welcoming hug.

After saying hello, everyone chatted while unloading the car.

o oo oooo oooooooo oooo oo

It was past noon by the time
they got finished settling in.

Mya looked around, but
surprisingly saw nothing to eat.
Her belly grumbled.

Memaw usually had some
sort of delicious *Cajun*
or *Creole* dish prepared,
but not this time.

o oo oooo ooooooo oooo oo

Cajun and Creole are both styles of cooking that originated in Louisiana, and jambalaya was Mya's favorite.

Jambalaya is mostly seasoned rice, mixed with shrimp and meat, like chicken, sausage, and pork.

o oo oooo ooooooo oooo oo

o oo oooo oooooooo oooo oo o

And now, Mya
was craving it.

o oo oooo oooooooo oooo oo

She looked around again.

. . . .

Nothing.

Memaw figured they'd be
hungry after their long drive,
but chose not to cook anything.

Instead, she decided to wait.
She knew how much Mya
enjoyed helping her in the kitchen.

o oo oooo ooooooo oooo oo

But Mya didn't know that.

She was hungry now!

"Can we go out for lunch

in the French Quarter?"

Mya asked.

The **French Quarter** is the

oldest neighborhood in **New**

Orleans, and also the city's

most popular tourist attraction.

o oo oooo ooooooo oooo oo

Mya loved going to the French Market whenever she was near the French Quarter.

o oo oooo ooooooo oooo oo

She learned how it was once a trading post for the Native Americans, and how it is now one of America's oldest public markets.

Mya also had fun watching street performers entertain crowds at Jackson Square, near the St. Louis Cathedral.

o oo oooo oooooooo oooo oo

· · · · · · ·

The great fire of 1794 caused the
original cathedral to burn down.

It was later rebuilt

sometime in the 1850s.

○ ○○ ○○○○ ○○○○○○○○ ○○○○ ○○

Memaw interrupted Mya's
French Quarter daydream

by replying with a
question of her own.

"Would you like to help me
make a big pot of gumbo
for everyone instead?"

Mya smiled,
"That's even better!"

o oo oooo oooooooo oooo oo

Gumbo is a popular dish
in the Southern states,
especially in *Louisiana*.

It is like soup,

but also like stew.

It's unique because

it is a flavorful

combination of both!

Memaw and Mya went

into the kitchen to gather

all ingredients needed

for the recipe.

o oo oooo oooooooo oooo oo

"First, we will make the roux."

Memaw instructed.

o oo oooo oooooooo oooo oo

"What's a roux?"

Mya asked.

"Roux is used to thicken the gumbo's gravy, usually by mixing flour and melted butter or oil together." She explained.

o oo oooo ooooooo oooo oo

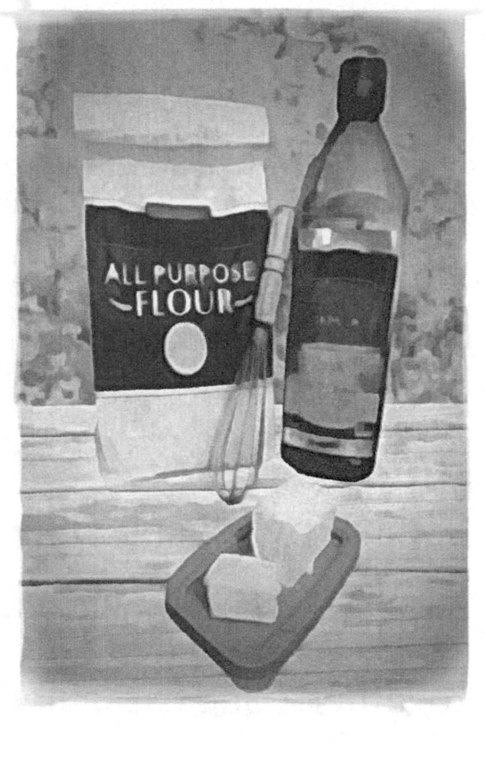
ALL PURPOSE
FLOUR

They began cooking the chicken and sausage on the stove while the roux simmered.

"Now, let's cut the chicken and sausage into smaller pieces to add into the roux."

o oo oooo oooooooo oooo oo o

Shrimp, okra, bell peppers, onions, garlic, celery, salt, and black pepper were also added.

o oo oooo oooooooo oooo oo

. . . .

"Gumbo has lots of ingredients!"

Mya said in amazement.

o oo oooo ooooooooo oooo oo

A separate pot of rice was made

to go with the gumbo as well.

Now, the kitchen smelled great!

o oo oooo ooooooo oooo oo o

When everything was finished,

Memaw smiled in delight.

As she stirred the pot, she
noted,

"Life is like gumbo."

o oo oooo ooooooo oooo oo

She looked at
Mya to explain.

"The roux is like our planet.
And the ingredients are like
the people on Earth. They are all
different colors, shapes, and sizes,
with their own individual flavors."

o oo oooo oooooooo oooo oo o

Still stirring, she continued,
"The gumbo wouldn't taste
very good without its roux
and added ingredients.

o oo oooo oooooooo oooo oo

But combined, they make it complete."

After listening to what Memaw said, Mya thought for a moment.

"I get it!" She exclaimed.

"The Earth is a much better place for everyone living on it when they are kind to one another by working together."

o oo oooo ooooooo oooo oo

Memaw nodded in agreement.

. . . .

"Just like gumbo."

She repeated.

"Now, let's eat!"

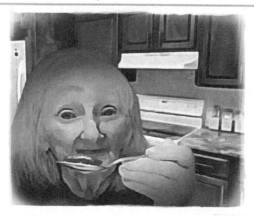

o oo oooo ooooooo oooo oo

o oo oooo oooooooo oooo oo

ABOUT THE AUTHOR

Marsha Parish was raised by
her loving and supportive
great-grandmother, down by the
bayou in Southeastern Louisiana,
until Hurricane Katrina in 2005.

She still happily resides in the
same state, on the outskirts of
New Orleans, with her son.

Parish doesn't usually write stories,
but here's to her first one, and
hopefully, many more to come!

o oo oooo   oooooooo oooo oo

ACKNOWLEDGMENTS

Writing a story based on southern living was truly an enjoyable, yet relatable experience. It was easily accomplished because of my own adventures and memories I share with my grandmother, Evelyn Perez.

She's the muse who aspires me in all that I do.

Thank you for everything,
Memaw.

o oo oooo ooooooo oooo oo

To my family and friends.

Thanks for finding the time to read through my rough drafts, and for giving honest opinions afterwards. Because of your good reviews, I decided to go forward and publish my work. You know who you are! Thank you.

Speaking of publishing, I'd like to thank Karissa for putting the idea in my head, and getting me started on this journey.

o oo oooo ooooooooo oooo oo

Susie, thank you
for promoting my work and
urging others to check it out.

Special thanks to Lindsey for
helping when it came to editorial
support. I appreciate it!

Sierra, thank you for reading
this story to the students in
your classroom.

To Ashlie and Tiffany:
Your opinions, suggestions, and
encouraging words meant the most
to me. You made me feel like I
could reach the sky. Thank you.

o oo oooo ooooooo oooo oo

And last,

but certainly not least...

Elijah:

My sweet boy,

I saved the best for last.

You were the first to

read my story.

Thank you for your input, for

believing in me, and for being

my number one fan.

Whenever I begin to doubt myself,

you're always there, reassuring

me. Without you, I'd be lost.

o oo oooo ooooooo oooo oo

In life, everyone has a person. I'm forever grateful that you're mine!

Your presence makes me, my life, and this world so much better…

just like gumbo.

I love you, son!

o oo oooo ooooooo oooo oo

Made in the USA
Coppell, TX
08 September 2022

82773097R30046